CARING FOR OUR FORESTS

Written by
Azra Limbada

New York

Published in 2022 by Cavendish Square Publishing, LLC
29 East 21st Street
New York, NY 10010

© 2020 Booklife Publishing
This edition is published by arrangement with Booklife Publishing

No part of this publication may be reproduced, stored in a retrieval system, or transmitted in any form or by any means—electronic, mechanical, photocopying, recording, or otherwise—without the prior permission of the copyright owner. Request for permission should be addressed to Permissions, Cavendish Square Publishing, 29 East 21st Street, New York, NY 10010. Tel (877) 980-4450; fax (877) 980-4454.

Website: cavendishsq.com

This publication represents the opinions and views of the author based on his or her personal experience, knowledge, and research. The information in this book serves as a general guide only. The author and publisher have used their best efforts in preparing this book and disclaim liability rising directly or indirectly from the use and application of this book.

All websites were available and accurate when this book was sent to press.

Edited by: John Wood
Designed by: Drue Rintoul

Cataloging-in-Publication Data
Names: Limbada, Azra.
Title: Caring for our forests / Azra Limbada.
Description: New York : Cavendish Square, 2022. | Series: Our planet, our future | Includes glossary and index.
Identifiers: ISBN 9781502663450 (pbk.) | ISBN 9781502663474 (library bound) | ISBN 9781502663467 (6 pack) | ISBN 9781502663481 (ebook)
Subjects: LCSH: Forest protection--Juvenile literature. | Forest conservation--Juvenile literature. | Environmental responsibility--Juvenile literature.
Classification: LCC SD411.L563 2022 | DDC 578.73--dc23

Some of the images in this book illustrate individuals who are models. The depictions do not imply actual situations or events.

CPSIA compliance information: Batch #CW22CSQ: For further information contact Cavendish Square Publishing LLC, New York, New York, at 1-877-980-4450.

Printed in the United States of America

CONTENTS

Page 4   **EARTH**

Page 6   **FORESTS**

Page 8   **OXYGEN AND CARBON DIOXIDE**

Page 10   **LIVING IN THE FOREST**

Page 12   **TREES**

Page 14   **DEFORESTATION**

Page 16   **FOREST FIRES**

Page 18   **MINING**

Page 20   **ISRA HIRSI**

Page 22   **MAKE YOUR OWN RECYCLED WIND CHIMES**

Page 24   **GLOSSARY AND INDEX**

> Words that look like this can be found in the glossary on page 24.

EARTH

We live on Earth. Our planet is about 4.5 billion years old. It is home to all sorts of living things. Life can be found everywhere, from steamy jungles to dry deserts.

EARTH

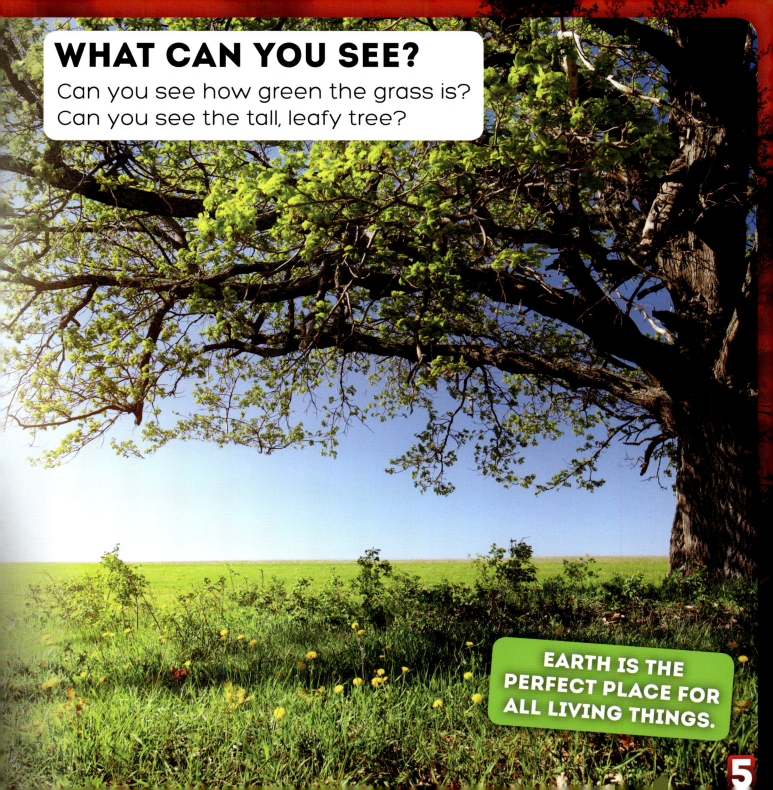

WHAT CAN YOU SEE?

Can you see how green the grass is?
Can you see the tall, leafy tree?

EARTH IS THE PERFECT PLACE FOR ALL LIVING THINGS.

FORESTS

A forest is made up of lots of different trees. Many animals live in forests and need them in order to stay alive.

WOODS ARE OFTEN SMALLER THAN FORESTS.

The Amazon is the largest rain forest in the world. A rain forest has lots of rain every year. There are millions of different species living in the Amazon.

OXYGEN AND CARBON DIOXIDE

Oxygen is all around us. It is a colorless <u>gas</u> that we need to stay alive. Every time we breathe in, we are taking in oxygen. Plants and trees make oxygen.

ALMOST ALL LIVING THINGS NEED OXYGEN.

Carbon dioxide is in the air that we breathe out. Trees and plants need carbon dioxide to grow. This means animals and plants <u>rely</u> on each other.

OXYGEN

CARBON DIOXIDE

WE NEED THE TREES AND THEY NEED US!

LIVING IN THE FOREST

Did you know that lots of people live in forests too? These people rely on trees and forests for their food and shelter.

MANY PEOPLE WHO LIVE IN THE RAIN FORESTS ARE INVOLVED IN TRYING TO PROTECT THEM.

Animals also need the forest to live. Animals such as sloths and monkeys use tall trees for shelter and to hide from their predators.

SLOTH

TREES

We use trees for lots of things. Wood from trees can be used to make houses. We also get lots of our medicine and food from trees.

IT IS IMPORTANT TO REPLACE THE TREES WE CUT DOWN BY PLANTING MORE.

DEFORESTATION

Deforestation is when trees in forests are cut down. Cutting down trees without planting new ones is bad for the <u>environment</u>.

DEFORESTATION ALSO MEANS THAT ANIMAL <u>HABITATS</u> ARE DESTROYED.

ONE WAY THAT YOU CAN HELP IS BY PLANTING TREES.

You can help stop deforestation by being responsible and reusing things that are made from trees, such as paper.

15

FOREST FIRES

A forest fire might be started by something in nature, such as a lightning strike. However, most forest fires are caused by humans.

Forest fires destroy habitats and add to the pollution around us. Sadly, it often takes a long time for a forest to recover from a fire.

FOREST FIRES ARE OFTEN CAUSED BY CAMPFIRES. REMEMBER TO ALWAYS BE SAFE WITH YOUR CAMPFIRE!

MINING

Mining is when humans dig deep into the ground to get things such as metals and coal. Coal is used to make electricity, but it causes lots of pollution.

COAL

Lots of trees are cut down before mining can happen. Mining can also pollute the ground or water nearby, killing even more plants and trees.

ISRA HIRSI

This is Isra Hirsi. She is an <u>activist</u> who is trying to stop <u>climate change</u>. Isra wants everyone to work together to help protect our planet.

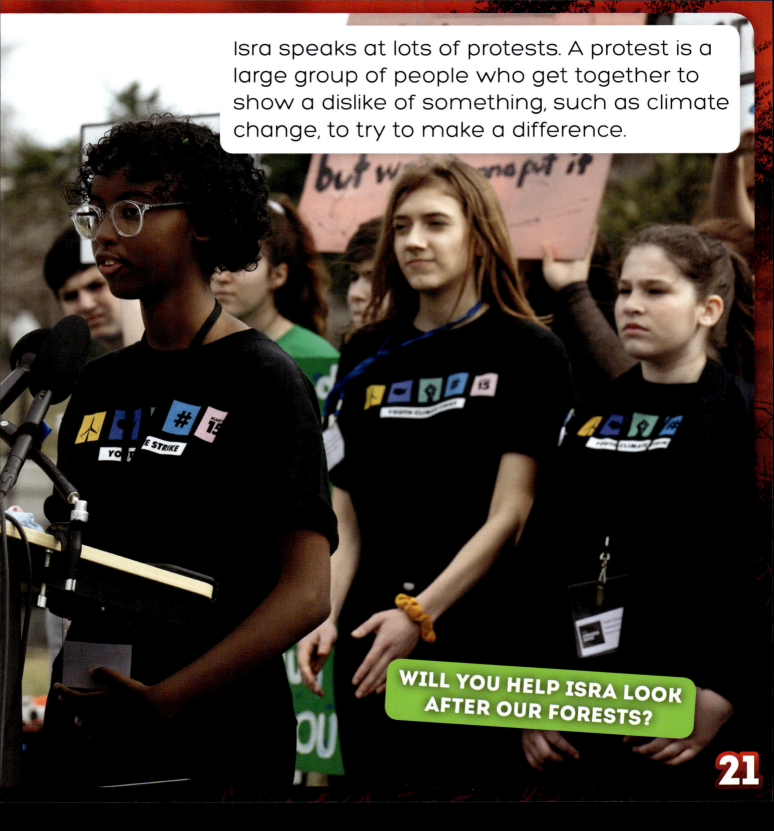

Isra speaks at lots of protests. A protest is a large group of people who get together to show a dislike of something, such as climate change, to try to make a difference.

WILL YOU HELP ISRA LOOK AFTER OUR FORESTS?

MAKE YOUR OWN RECYCLED WIND CHIMES

Here's everything you need to make your own recycled wind chimes.

CLEAN CANS

WASHABLE PAINT

STRING

TAPE

METAL WASHERS (You'll have to ask an adult to help you find these!)

STEP 1: Paint the outside of your cans. Once they are dry, ask an adult to make a hole in the bottom of the cans.

STEP 2: Push string through the holes.

STEP 3: Tie some washers along one end of the string, inside the cans. They will hold the string in place and make noise.

STEP 4: Hang the cans outside using tape. When the wind blows, they will make a lovely sound.

GLOSSARY

activist	someone who tries to make a change by speaking out
climate change	a change in the typical weather or temperature of a large area
environment	the natural world
gas	a thing that is like air, which spreads out to fill any space available
habitats	the natural homes in which animals, plants, and other living things live
pollution	something added to our environment that is harmful to living things
predators	animals that hunt other animals for food
recycle	to use again to make something else
rely	to trust or depend on something
species	a group of very similar animals or plants that can create young together

INDEX

activists 20
animals 6, 9, 11, 14
carbon dioxide 9
climate change 20-21
deforestation 14-15

forests 6-7, 10-11, 14, 16-17, 21
habitats 14, 17
oxygen 8
pollution 17-19